chapter
one

I wave and leave the stage. Cole offers me his arm and helps me down the ramp that leads to the dressing room, which in reality is a just fancy locker room. It's another sell-out crowd in one of the largest venues in the United States and I don't remember a single moment of it. I'm not ungrateful for what's been afforded to me, but I'm bitter. The title of *America's Sweetheart* has run its course, and there isn't anything I can do about it. It's not the fans' faults, or even my manager's. I can't blame the media or the record label. The blame falls solely on my shoulders and those of my ex-fiancé, Ryan Stone. Except he doesn't accept any blame for the demise of our five year relationship.

My personal assistant and best friend extraordinaire, Alex, sits in my sunflower-filled dressing room rocking her newborn daughter. It's crazy how the relationship between Alex and Cole – who I also once dated – garners more headlines than

my being single for the past year. Ryan used to be a staple at my shows when we first got engaged. That was until his job became more and more important. I suppose the less the media saw of him, the less they cared. They just want to know how I can cope with the fact that my best friend married my ex and are both on tour with me. It's easy; Alex and Cole were meant to be together, and we're family.

Sitting down in front of the large mirror, I stare back at the woman I am now. Not too long ago, I thought of myself as a young girl, but that ship has sailed. I'm fighting gravity and losing the battle every day. The dark bags under my eyes aren't being cured by the cool cucumber slices I cover them with each and every morning. Gray hairs seem to rear their ugly heads seconds before a photo shoot, and the crow's feet are driving me nuts. I shouldn't look or feel this way, but that's what stress does.

When you lose the love of your life because you can't find a happy medium, because neither of you can compromise and because neither of you are willing to give up your careers, it causes an unhealthy amount of stress. Stress leads to the rapid aging process that I'm experiencing now.

I never thought I'd look in the mirror and be unhappy with what I see, but I am. Since Ryan left, the light in my eyes has been extinguished. The happiness in my smile is non-existent. Even when I walk, it's without a purpose. Everyone experiences break-ups differently. Some need them in order to grow up, while others need them to escape and find themselves. I'm not sure what Ryan and I needed, except for time to stop so we could figure out what was going on. By the time either of us did, he was living in Boston and I was in New York about to embark on an eighteen-month tour with no word on whether he'd join me at any of the stops.

When your relationship is ending, you try everything you can think of to keep it together. You both make promises that neither of you can keep. Words are said that can never be taken back. Emotions are worn on your sleeve and your partner sees your pain. Your wants and needs become the "be all that ends all", but they only work if they're met. When you want a family

and are ready to settle down but have to repeatedly change your wedding date due to the demands of your record label, your partner withdraws. The phone calls become few and far between. You resort to texting and its one-word answers. In the end you give up, even if you don't mean to.

Most of the time, you don't realize what's going on around you until it's too late. I should've seen the signs – they're what make my songs so popular. I sing about true love, finding romance and experiencing heartbreak. I should've known. I was too naïve to think that if we made it through a break-up before we'd survive anything. Once my tour was over, we'd fix everything.

It's been a year since I've spoken to Ryan Stone. Twelve months since he called and said that things aren't working and that we wanted different things in life. I wanted children, he didn't. He wanted me not to tour during baseball season, I did. Three hundred and sixty-five days since he told me that he'll always love me, but that he was staying in Boston and accepting the job of General Manager of the major league baseball team, the Boston Renegades.

I glance into the mirror at Alex as she feeds her daughter. It's hard not to be jealous of her, but I am. I could be her right now, but I chose to be alone. Cole wanted to get back together, to make a go of things, but I wasn't in a good place in my life. I had just given up Ryan, for his own good, and needed to figure out a few things. A year with a therapist did that and while I was getting my head shrunk, Cole was falling in love with my best friend. Truth be told, I didn't care. They fit together, but it's hard not to be jealous when she's holding the one thing I wanted Ryan and me to share and now never will.

I never thought the age difference would play a factor, but it did. In some ways, Ryan is still growing up, and being tied down to a wife and kids isn't where he is in life. It's where I'm at though and my clock is ticking, even more so now that Hayden is here and on tour. Every day I get to see my goddaughter and as much as I love her, I want my own. I want to feel the unconditional love for a child that I created with a man that I love. I want to hold him, rock him to sleep and be the first

thing he sees in the morning. My desire is much stronger now than it was a year ago and I know I can do this on my own, but I don't want to.

I've never, in the past nine years, stopped loving Ryan. To this day, I still wear my engagement ring. Maybe it's because I'm not mentally healthy enough to accept that he's gone or maybe I hope that he comes back. Neither answer is sufficient. I wear it because it reminds me of what I had and lost.

Cole comes into view and leans over Alex's shoulder. He gently touches Hayden and her little hand shoots out of her blanket, grabbing his finger. He laughs at his daughter all while Alex gazes lovingly at her husband, both oblivious that I'm in the room. Looking at their happy family unit only hits home how much I need a change in my life.

I clear my throat. "Alex, how many days until the next show?" I ask without making eye contact for fear she'll see what my eyes may tell her.

"You have five days. Why, what's up?"

I stand and square my shoulders. "I'm going to head home and see my parents. I'll meet you guys at the next stop, okay?" My voice is weak, and I can tell by her expression that she knows I'm up to something. I smile softly and walk toward my suitcase. She won't question me with Cole in the room so if I pack quickly, I can be gone before the inquisition starts.

"You okay, Hadley girl?"

I nod, unable to answer Cole. He won't pester me and for that I'm thankful. With my bag packed, I tell them goodbye and walk down the long corridor until I'm standing outside the venue. No one is expecting me to be outside, and I rather enjoy walking undetected with fans still trying to get out of the parking lot. I flag down a taxi and slide in the back, memories of me doing this so many years ago flashing before my eyes. I know I'm doing the right thing.

"Airport, please."

chapter
two

RYAN

My chair leans back as I stare through my floor-to-ceiling windows onto the field. It's a practice day and from what I can see, no one is really taking it seriously. My watch indicates that practice has just started, reminding me to give the manager more leeway than my predecessor. I told myself when I took this job that I'm not going to be *that guy*, the "young, gung-ho fresh-out-of-college kid who's been called in to do something with the team" guy. That's not me. At least that's not my intention. I want to win and will do so at whatever cost without damaging the integrity of the team.

I spin in my chair and face my desk. It's clear of all the paperwork that cluttered it not weeks before. Now that the season is in full swing I can take a little reprieve and enjoy the sport I've grown to love so much. I eye my college diploma, which now hangs proudly on my wall. Going back to school

was the smartest decision I've made during these past few years. I struggled, of course, but was able to take most of my classes online while still working for the Yankees'. Management encouraged my continuing education, but I don't think they planned on me leaving for their rival.

I started with the *Renegades* part way through last year. They were in last place and the former General Manager let the team go to shit. It was more like watching misfits play stickball than major league baseball. There was drinking in the clubhouse, escorts who loitered in the VIP section and a lot of marriages were crumbling.

Mine crumbled long before I got here though. Not that I was married, but I was damn near close. I should've been at least three times, by all accounts, with as many dates that were set, but we never made it down the aisle. Hell, we never even made it to the tux shop or sent out invites. I supposed with the lack of finality, no one's in a hurry to do anything. It's easy to change the date when no one knows you've set one.

My ex-fiancée is who every teenage boy dreams of falling in love with. When I met Hadley Carter, I was seventeen, lost and very impressionable. My home life sucked, I had exactly one friend and I was destined to work in the same mill that the Stone men before me had worked. Hadley opened my eyes to a whole new world and she also broke my heart. Our relationship, which was kept hidden, was a whirlwind of love, emotions and secrets. It was the secrets that came back to destroy us. Hadley is a major recording artist. Her concerts sell out within hours, her label loves her and she's in high demand, so high that it cost us our relationship.

It took four years until I saw her again in the flesh. One random night I was out with my friends and there she was, standing a few feet from me. That same night, we reconnected and I knew I wanted to spend the rest of my life with her.

I knew that up until a year ago when I was offered the interim GM job with Boston, I jumped on it. We needed something different and I thought she would be happy. I wanted her to quit touring for a bit, set a wedding date and let us be married for a while. Turns out, my plan was not the same

as her plan. She went on tour and I moved here.

I thought she'd follow or at least move her belongings to my new condo, but she didn't. After a while, you just stop trying. I know I did. I couldn't find time to call her at midnight when her shows were over, and I didn't want to wake her up by calling too early. Our schedules didn't mesh. I got busy and so did she.

Breaking up with the one you love is life changing. How I came to that decision, I'll never know. Deep down, I knew Hadley would've never done it and more than likely pretended that everything was okay with us, but I couldn't. My life was split in half. One part of me wanted to give up the life I was building before she came back and tour with her. I tried that, in the off-season, but it wasn't the life for me. Back when we first met, I broke every rule ever set for me just to be with her. She showed me what it was like to have a glamorous life and for the longest time, I could see myself following her around. Sure, at seventeen, I didn't know what I wanted, except for her. She was everything I wanted. When she broke up with me, my life took a different path. My parents weren't going to pay for my college, and at the time, I wasn't even living at home due to them finding out about my relationship with Hadley. My best friend, Dylan, and I moved to New York City. I took every business class I could at a community college while working a job to help keep Dylan and me in an apartment. Everything paid off, and I landed a dream job with the Yankees. Then Hadley walked back into my life. It was happenstance. We were both in the right place at the time right time. I never looked back after that night. Until now.

The other part of me wanted Hadley to stop performing, not stop singing. Sadly for me, those go hand in hand. I wanted us to have time to build a life together without touring being in the way. We lived by her calendar and while I have a busy schedule, mine at least afforded us vacation time.

For the first year, she didn't tour and didn't release anything new. Life was perfect. We spent our first Christmas in Cancun surrounded by pristine beaches and the warm sun. It wasn't until we'd been together for two and half years did

our schedules really start to impact our lives. We both worked long hours, we both traveled and we both forgot about each other. Hadley thought that we should have a child, said it would bring us closer and we'd be forced to make changes to our work schedules. I said no. I told her that I wasn't ready and that a baby shouldn't be used as a pawn for us to make changes.

Being offered the job in Boston was eye opening. Hadley doesn't have to live in New York so I didn't think it would be a big deal. I thought we'd move, maybe buy a house and really start making plans. When I first pitched the idea to her, she seemed to be on board, but that quickly changed when she told me she was going on an eighteen-month tour and wanted me to quit and go with her. When I told her no, she blew it off saying she wouldn't be gone the entire time and would have a month off between her international and US dates, together with some long weekends. I didn't know if that was her way of saying everything would be okay or not. It wasn't for me. I still expected her to move with me to Boston. If you're about to spend the next year and half on the road, what's it matter where your physical address is?

It's not in Boston, which was evident when I started showing her condos to rent. She told me she wanted to stay in New York because of work. Her studio, manager and label were there and it was convenient. For the first time since I was seventeen, I cried. I wanted her with me. I needed her with me. Even having her clothes or stupid high-heels in our bedroom was better than anything.

Eventually, I made the conscious decision to move. If she wasn't going to be home there was no need for me to stay. She promised everything would be fine. It was just a tour and once it was over, we'd be back together. Except life doesn't work like that and now we're not together.

When we broke up, I expected to find our demise splashed all over *Page Six*, but it wasn't. Her publicist never released a statement. I don't know if that was for my benefit or hers. When I see her in magazines and on television, because I have to torture myself, she still wears the ring I put on her finger

so many years ago. Why she still does, I'll never know, nor will I find out. It's been a year since we've spoken, since she begged me not to do this to us. I had to. I had to make the best decision for me.

It's hard to make a life-altering decision, but when I think about it, each conscious decision you make is life altering. Whether you make a change in your daily routine, leave your house five minutes late or start dating the boss' daughter, your life has changed.

Six months ago, I took a step that I wasn't sure I'd be able to take and started seeing Jessica Robertson, daughter of Mitch Robinson, owner of the Boston Renegades. She pursued me, with her father's blessing, and she knows everything about Hadley and me. The difference in my relationship with Jessica is that we date. We go out and talk, see movies and let our relationship progress naturally. With Hadley, everything happened so fast – most of it in secret – and we never really had the chance to be a normal couple.

Dating Jessica is easy. She grew up with her father not being at home during the season. She loves baseball and doesn't mind being at the stadium. To her, a baseball life is second nature and that fits in with who I am right now.

Most importantly, she knows I'm still in love with Hadley.

chapter
three

S tanding outside the grand ballpark, it hits me like a ton of bricks that I never visited Ryan at work. I don't know why. I guess I didn't need to. Living in the same city, I never found the urge to surprise him at work. Looking back now, I see that was a mistake on my part. I've heard so many romantic stories about spur-of-the-moment lunches or walks in the park. Maybe he was right in breaking up with me. I can't remember if I actually made time for "us" outside of living together.

As soon as I step inside the concourse, my heart races and my palms start to sweat. I'm not a nervous person by nature, but knowing that I'm about to see Ryan for the first time in a year has me on edge. As many times as I've been in stadiums, I've never been on the concourse. I've never been to a major sporting event or another concert as a fan. In this moment, I feel as if I've missed out on an important American pastime.

There are food vendors of every food imaginable lining both sides. Every few openings are spots where you can buy game gear. Ryan's closet was full of gear and I often teased him that he had nothing fancy except for a tuxedo. My heels tap loudly against the concrete floor as I traverse down the hall looking for a sign that will tell me how to find his office. This is something I should've done with Ryan when he first started working here. I should've made the time to check out his office and meet his co-workers, but I didn't. The more I think about my actions during the break-up, the more I'm convinced that I'm shallow and unworthy of his love. I know deep down that isn't true, but walking these halls while I look for his office sure makes me feel that way.

"Can I help you?"

I turn to see an older man behind me. He's dressed in a baseball uniform and it dawns on me that today might be a game day. I never stopped to check. Ryan may be too busy to talk to me. He may suggest I come back at a different time, knowing that my schedule is tight and that flexibility is not my best friend. The man stares at me. His eyes aren't roaming around my body in a perverted sense, but he knows that I don't belong here. I smile, hoping to ease his worries. I have no doubt the players get all kinds of stalkers and people trying to break into the locker room. I'm only trying to find their boss.

"I'm looking for Ryan Stone's office."

His gaze turns sharp and now I have no doubt he's looking at me as if I'm some sort of psycho. I may have ignored Ryan's career move, but I do know he's the youngest general manager in baseball history and he's single – a prize to any woman looking for that better fish in the sea. I should know. I caught him. Twice.

"Mr. Stone is a very busy man," he says with a thick Boston accent. It's always amazed me how different the dialects are from New York to Boston. We're so close, only a few hundred miles separating us, yet we're so different.

"I have no doubt, but I need to see him. Is there someone I can talk to that may be able to call him?"

"You don't have his number?" he asks a very valid question.

Yes, I have his number, but I'm hoping for the element of surprise. My ideal situation puts me in the general vicinity of his office where I can be announced and he can't run from me. Cell phones can be ignored and calls sent to voicemail. I don't want to give him that option.

I pull my phone out of my purse and wave it at him. I contemplate giving him my story, telling him who I am, but my status was never important to Ryan. He never once asked me to sing the National Anthem at one of the games or asked me to donate to a charity dinner. I gladly held his arm at many, but was always introduced as Hadley Carter, fiancée. I know that I can tell this man who I am and use a sentence like, "shall I have my publicist call Mr. Stone's secretary", but that doesn't accomplish what I'm here to do.

I take a deep breath and prepare for this old man's eyes to widen. Clearing my throat, I square my shoulders and grin. "I'm Mr. Stone's ex-fiancée. I'm passing through town, and I thought I'd surprise him."

His eyes do in fact widen, and it's neither a good nor bad thing. He either realizes who I am from the tabloids or maybe from Ryan, but I doubt the latter. Ryan was never a gossip, especially about us. Dylan was though, and I'm sure she still is. However, most people know who I am. I've been around long enough to make some type of impact on one's memory. Or it's a bad sign. I said the words 'ex-fiancée' and this man knows nothing about me.

"May I see some ID?" he asks, shuffling his feet forward.

I appease him by pulling out my wallet and opening it for him. His eyes widen again and he steps back. "If you walk down this way, take a left and head up the escalator, you'll find his office is about half way down the hall on the left-hand side. Someone should be able to buzz you in."

"Thank you very much," I say with as much gratitude as I can muster. Knowing that I'm close and about to see him, my heart is pounding through my chest.

"My granddaughter loves your music, Miss Carter."

His words warm me and I reach into my bag and pull out a piece of paper. "What's her name?"

"Sylvia," he replies as I write out a note to her, telling her that she has a wonderful grandfather. I hand it him and his eyes glass over.

"Thank you so much."

"Do you have a phone?"

He nods and pulls it out of his pocket. I reach for it and step close to him, putting my arm around him. We smile for the epic fan selfie and I can feel the excitement coming from him. If I had to guess, he's around major league ball players every day, but he's excited to be standing next to me.

"There ya go, now you can show Sylvia."

"Thank you again," he graciously says, staring at his phone.

"You're welcome, and thank you for the directions." Without waiting for his reply, I speedily walk in the direction he's sent me. I hurry up the escalator and down the hall until I see his office. He's done so well for himself, and I wish I could say I had a part in it. I didn't. I could've had a part in his failure, but he was stronger than me. He always has been.

I try the door out of habit and am surprised to find it open. The heart pounding that I was experiencing downstairs is nothing like what's going on now. A shortness of breath over takes me as I step in. It's quiet and the carpeted floor muffles my shoes. There are three offices and one grand reception desk that's currently empty. Two of the offices have closed doors and one is open. I take my chance and hope that this is Ryan's office.

Walking to the last office on the left, I catch a glimpse of the ball field. Yes, of course this would be his office; he is, after all, the boss. I hear faint voices the closer I get and hope that I'm not interrupting him in a meeting. If I am, I resolve myself to sit in reception and wait for him to finish. Now that I'm here and he's this close, I'm not leaving until I speak with him. He may not have much to say, but I do.

I step into his doorway and immediately feel like I'm being hit by a truck. His arms are wrapped around a woman, a brunette. She's the complete opposite of me. She leans in, kissing him and he kisses her back. My hand clutches the doorjamb as my breathing intensifies. We've been broken up a

year and he's already moved on. I haven't even thought about another person except for him, let alone entertain the idea of moving on. I can't because I'm still in love with him. When I close my eyes at night, he's all I see.

My options are limited. I can walk back to reception, take a seat and wait patiently, or I can stand tall and act like what I'm seeing doesn't affect me, regardless of the pain that's ricocheting through me right now.

I clear my throat and they break apart. Ryan's eyes go wide, but his hands don't move from her waist. She turns and looks at me, a soft smile spreading across her lips. Does she know about me? She leans forward and places a kiss on his cheek before removing herself from his arms. He's frozen in place, his eyes locked on mine.

The woman passes me, smiling again as she walks out of the room. If I were she, I probably would've brushed my shoulder against hers, but she doesn't and that makes her the better person. I'm seeing nothing but green right now. The jealousy and rage I'm feeling is circumventing my ability to talk and move.

Ryan rests against the back of his chair, his hand covering his mouth. Is he wiping away the kisses he just shared hoping that there's no evidence or that I didn't see them? I could yell and scream, show how hurt I am, but we aren't together. I have no right, but damn it if my heart isn't breaking all over again.

"What are you doing here, Hadley?"

chapter
four

In a million years, I never thought I'd find Hadley Carter standing in my doorway with the fakest smile I've ever seen pasted across her face. Yet, here she is, pretending to be as cordial as ever, when I know deep inside her the jealousy is raging. I have to give Jessica credit. She knew the moment that Hadley cleared her throat that we needed privacy, although I wouldn't have faulted her for staying either. She has every right to. She and I are together and trying to build a relationship. I think some women would benefit from Jessica's confidence in this situation. I would assume if guys were more honest with their feelings, their lives might be a bit less complicated. Lucky for me, Jessica knew about my relationship and break-up and was there to lend an ear. I'm the one who made the first move.

Hadley's hands are clutched together, making me curious if it's out of anger or nervousness. I'm wondering if there's some new TV reality show filming awkward reunions

standing behind her waiting to bust in the room and shove a microphone in my face. I wouldn't put it past her to sign up for some show like that. She's a junkie when it comes to reality TV, but I would like to think that she has more respect for me and our past than to do something like that.

I lean back in my chair and cover my mouth to… what? Stifle a groan? Hide the shock? Either reaction to Hadley standing in my doorway is possible. My back is rigid as the tension in my body starts to take over. It's three hours before game time and the guys will be taking to the field for batting practice. I don't need to be there, but I like to watch. I like knowing that everything's being taken seriously. It's hard to instill authority when you're as young or younger than most of the team.

"What do you want, Hadley?" My words are terse, causing her to step back slightly. I don't know how I feel with her here. Why is she here? Why didn't she just call? I try to recall whether or not I know her schedule or when it was that I stopped caring. I can't answer that. I look her up. I follow her. Hell, I'm probably a stalker in most peoples' eyes. It's a morbid curiosity that I have.

For the longest time, I didn't know anything about her. I didn't want to. Dylan helped by keeping me away from the tabloids, and we were always so busy that we never watched television. Once Hadley and I got back together, I knew not to read the tabloids even though they were good to her. Of course, we were front-page news for a bit, but that quickly died down. Neither of us were party-goers. We were boring to them, and that was just fine with us.

Yet, they still think we're together or maybe they don't and just don't care. It's not like Jessica and I have a media draw, and Hadley's been on tour. I suppose if someone were following me, they'd be splashing my philandering all over the media. Either that or Hadley's publicist is making sure none of it gets out until the tour is over, and I'm painted as the bad guy who broke the heart of America's Sweetheart.

If only they knew.

The ring I gave her glimmers with sunlight shining through

my window. I try not to gaze at the sparkler, but I can't help myself. I was so proud the day I purchased that diamond for her. I couldn't wait to slip it onto her finger. Dylan begged me not to. She pleaded with me to change my mind, but I didn't listen. I thought we'd get married, have a few kids and live a peaceful, yet exciting life. Boy was I wrong.

I clear my throat and swivel my chair toward the window. I can't look at her for fear that she'll cry or bat her eyelashes, and I'll go running. She looks amazing, better than before she left for her tour. Not seeing her for the last year has done a number on my memories.

"I had to see you." Her normally sweet voice is barely audible. I bring my hand to my head, rubbing my temple and forehead. The impending headache will likely be a killer and will either make or break my night.

"Why? It's only been a year," I state matter-of-factly. I know she knows this, but I can't help but get the jab in. It was so easy for her to quit on us, as if we never meant anything to each other.

"That's why I'm here."

From the corner of my eye I see her cautious steps into my office. I move slightly and watch her take in my office. I wanted her here when I started, but she was too busy. Always busy. My life never took precedence over her busy schedule.

"You have a nice office, Ryan. I never…" her voice trails off leaving me to wonder what she was going to say. She never what, thought I'd amount to anything? Didn't think I could make it on my own without her in my life? I clench my fist to curb the anger boiling inside of me. *This* conversation should've happened a year ago. She should've been here when the break-up happened, talking to me.

"Hadley, I'm going to ask you again, why are you here?" This time I turn and look at her, and it's a huge mistake. The urge to pull her into my arms is so great, but I can't act on it. I know she'll fall into my arms and let me hold her, but that's not fair to Jessica. I could never betray her like that.

Hadley walks toward me, her perfume growing stronger. I close my eyes and will away the images in my head, except

they don't go anywhere. They play out like a Ryan and Hadley movie on rewind, and I can't find the stop button. When I open my eyes, she's sitting across from me with her legs crossed and her hands clasped in her lap. She's ever the professional, and I'm falling apart here. I should be the strong one. I had to be when a decision had to be made about us. But looking at her now, she's the persona of someone who's confident and put together. She's on a mission and if I had to guess, it's to win me back.

"Ryan, I'm going to just blurt everything out. I'm assuming by the people working down on the field that it's game day so I'll be quick." Hadley pushes down her skirt, not that it moves one single solitary inch because I'm watching it like a hawk, but the gesture's there nonetheless. She looks at me, tilting her head until we make eye contact. Her smile is wide, and my face is pensive. I don't think I could smile if I wanted to right now.

She clears her throat and continues. "I should've done this a long time ago. I don't know if it was my pride, or utter shallowness that has kept me away, but I make no excuses. I have failed you and us one too many times and judging by what I walked in on, I know I'm too late. I don't deserve a second chance and I'm not here to ask for one, but I'd like to be friends. We never really had a friendship if you think about it. We met when you were so young, and I was completely smitten with you. It was a combination of romance, lust and hiding. You were my dirty little secret for the longest time. When you walked back into my life, we were given another chance, but it was right back to where we had left off that fateful night in the rental car. We never had a chance to be just friends, and I'd like that."

Her words stun me, and I hate that she's right. Dylan and I were friends before we crossed the line and are still friends, best friends at that. Hadley and I have only known each other as lovers. But I'm not sure I can do this with Hadley. I love her. Those feelings don't go away. I don't know what I'd do if she casually brushed against me, or put her hand on my arm to laugh at a joke. Those are all things that Dylan does and they have no effect on me, but if Hadley did touch me, I'd crumble.

"I don't know, Hadley," I push out the words even though I don't want to. "Being your friend right now will be hard. You're on tour, and I live here. What are you going to do, come visit me when you get a chance and act like nothing's wrong? We broke up. I ended our five-year relationship, and it's taken you a year to come and find me." I'm growing angrier by the minute and know that I need to calm down, but I can't. Standing up, I turn my attention to the window and look out onto the field. Guys are starting to warm-up, preparing for tonight's game.

"It's been a year and now you show up asking to be friends only because you saw that I'm with someone else? If you hadn't seen her, what would you be asking me? For a chance to get back together?"

"Ryan, I didn't come here to fight."

"Then why are you here?" I blast as I turn back to face her. She jumps slightly at my tone. "Why have you shown up after all this time? You don't call, text or even write, not that you did when we were together, and now you randomly show up in my office without warning?"

Hadley chokes back a sob, and it pains me to know that my telling her some home truth has caused her to cry. She shakes her head and wipes fiercely at her tears. "I miss you, that's why. I know it's a shitty excuse because I've been on tour, but it's all I have. After my show last night, everything just hit me. I'm alone and lost. Everything I had was gone, and I did it. I ruined everything because I don't know how to compromise."

I walk back to my desk, running my hand through my hair. Neither Hadley nor I had the ideal childhood. Hers was performance after performance and mine was trying to survive until I was old enough to move out. We grew up so differently, yet in so many ways we were the same, both searching for acceptance. Everything that I have, I've had to work for. Hadley, yes she's worked, but now everyone caters to her needs.

"Maybe you should call me when you're not on tour. We can't be friends for a night or two and then you disappear again. I can't do that." My voice is quiet and unsure.

"My tour's done. I cancelled my remaining shows."

My eyes find hers quickly, and I realize that I've just opened the door for her to waltz right back into my life. That's something I can't let happen.

chapter
five

The words were out of my mouth before I could stop them. By the look in his eyes, he wasn't expecting me to say that. Now I have to do the unthinkable, the unforgivable and cancel. I can't go back on tour now that I've told Ryan it's done. It's not going to be easy and there's going to be press. Carrie, my manager, isn't going to be happy. This is not me. I don't do things like this, but Ryan is important to me. Our relationship – or lack thereof – is important. The last thing I want is for people to know that Ryan and I aren't together. I've worked hard to keep up this ruse and I can't let a slip of the tongue burst my bubble. Unbeknownst to Ryan, I've just unleashed a whole slew of drama for him, and he's not going to like that.

I break his penetrating gaze and look out the window. There are people walking through the stands, but from where I sit, they look like blobs just moving aimlessly, or zombies

preparing to overtake the colony. I like the zombie analogy better. They can come get me and put me out of my misery. Someone's going to need to.

"How long have you been dating?" It's not a question I want to ask, but I need to know. The thought of dating never crossed my mind. I look down at my ring finger and move my engagement ring back and forth. Maybe if I had taken this off, dating wouldn't seem like such a foreign concept to me.

Ryan sighs heavily. He clears his throat, gathering my attention. When I look at him, I see confusion and hurt. His eyes aren't smiling, and his forehead is creased. I did this to him. The right thing to do would be to get up and leave, to forget that I was even here. I could stand and slip off my ring, place it on his desk and leave, but I'm not strong enough for a grand gesture like that.

"Hadley... I," he stops and rubs his face roughly with his hand. I want to reach out and pull his hand away and tell him that everything will be okay, that we'll be okay, but I don't even believe that myself. Once again, if I want Ryan, I'll be competing with another woman. First Dylan, and now this new one. Maybe that's my sign to step away.

"Her name's Jessica," he informs me without making eye contact. He picks something up off his desk, a paperclip I'm guessing, and starts to fiddle with it. "We've been dating for about six months." Ryan leans back in his chair and looks at me. "I didn't plan for it to happen; it just did. She's the owner's daughter, and we we're spending a lot of time together because we're close in age. She showed me around Boston and was my shoulder to cry on."

"She knows about me? I mean, she must because she left as soon as I made my presence known."

He nods. "Yes, she does. I told her everything."

"Why?" I have to ask even though I don't want to know the answer. I figured he'd talk to Dylan about us, not some stranger. I confided in Alex and thought that Ryan would at least talk to Cole. They had grown close over the years. Guess I was wrong once again.

"She's easy to talk to. She doesn't judge or care who you

are," he pauses to gauge my reaction. What does he want from me? Am I supposed to freak out that she doesn't care who I am? Right now, I don't really care because I'm having a hard enough time processing that he turned to another woman so quickly.

"I didn't mean it like that, Hadley. Of course she cares; it's just that she grew up with her own class of celebrities so it didn't really shock her when I told her. I think she knew about us anyway, and when you weren't around or I didn't talk about you, she asked. I spilled, and it felt good to talk to someone about everything."

"You had Cole. You haven't talked to him since you moved to Boston."

Ryan shakes his head. "Cole belongs to you. He was only my friend by association. I have Dylan, but she didn't want to hear anything I had to say."

"She still hates me."

He shrugs, all but confirming what I've known for years. A quick silence washes over the room. We haven't had an awkward moment like this since the night we met. His phone buzzes, causing us both to jump.

"Yeah?" he says after picking up the receiver. "All right, I'll be down in a minute." After he hangs up, he stands and buttons his suit jacket. My eyes are downcast, knowing that our meeting is about to come to an end, and I don't know what I'm going to do to ensure I can see him again. I can't just show up tomorrow.

"I have to go," he says when he stops in front of me. I acknowledge him, but only slightly. "I'll walk you out."

"Can I see you tomorrow?" I ask him. I want to reach out and pull his hand into mine, but the thought of rejection pains me so much that I don't think I'd make it out of this room if that were to happen.

Ryan's lips form into a fine line as he shakes his head. "I don't think that's such a good idea, Hadley."

"Why not?" I bite back the cry that's building in my throat.

He runs his hand through his hair, pulling on the ends. "I don't know. Things are good for me here, and I'm not going

anywhere. I asked you to move here, but you didn't. We broke up. Twelve months later and now you're standing in my office? Honestly, I'm a bit confused, and I need some time to think."

I set my hand on his arm and gently pull his hand away from his hair. I don't let go and allow my fingers to linger against his skin. The spark is still there, it's never gone away. I still feel the same as I did the first night we met as he held me under the stars. He was so innocent then.

"Friends, remember?"

There's a moment of hesitation before he nods.

"Well as your friend, I'd like to see you tomorrow. I know you work crazy hours so just tell me when and where we can meet and I'll be there." I turn and leave knowing it's a long shot, but I figure if I leave him with those words, he doesn't have time to formulate a response that will end with him telling me to get lost.

I rush out of his office and back through the halls that led me to him, holding back the tears. I won't cry here. I can't. As soon as I'm outside, my phone is pressed to my ear. I meander into the crowd, who are likely here to attend the game tonight, and keep my head low.

"Hadley, where the hell are you?"

"Carrie, I'm in Boston." Carrie's my manager and has been since I fired my uncle Ian. Firing him wasn't easy, but career wise, it was in my best interests. Ian did some very shady things behind the scenes and made me look like something I wasn't. He was also the catalyst that destroyed Ryan and I the first time.

"Come again?"

I pause and gather my bearings. Carrie's been good to me over the years and I'm about to put her in a horrible spot. I wouldn't be surprised if she fires me and leaves me to hang from the gallows. It's what I deserve. "I'm in Boston. I flew here last night after the show and I can't leave anytime soon."

Carrie sighs and I can hear her moving around her office. The door slams, causing me to jump as if I'm sitting in the chair in front of her desk. "Okay, start from the beginning and tell me why you're in Boston."

"I just broke. I had to see him." I stand in the crowd,

waiting to cross the street. I shuffle along with everyone once the signal changes, signaling that it's clear to walk. "I can't finish the tour, Carrie."

"WHAT!?" she screeches. "You better be dying a slow painful death, Hadley Carter. The label will not stand for this."

I stop and take cover in a doorway. "I know, so postpone the rest of it. I can't finish it right now. My heart… it isn't with music right now. It'd be unfair to the fans for me to continue. I'd be letting them down night after night. I was so stupid a year ago that I lost everything, and now that I've seen him, I want him back. I *need* to do this for me."

"Hadley, sweetie, I know you're hurt and you never took the time after the break-up to allow yourself to heal, but we've been down this path with Ryan before. Remember when we first met? You were in therapy and doing so well getting over the relationship. You were healed. I know it's hard to swallow, but you've both grown up and your lives are vastly different. Cancelling your tour is unprecedented. My advice, finish the tour; he'll be there when you're done."

I shake my head, even though she can't see me. "He won't be. He's been dating someone for six months. Time is my enemy right now."

Carrie sighs, and I can hear papers being moved around and some incoherent mumbling in the background. "You and Ryan have too many differences. I wish you'd see that. You wanted a family. He wasn't ready. He wants a career. You wanted him with you. None of that has changed, Hadley. I'm afraid that you're going to ruin your career over this."

I know what she's saying is true. I could lose everything with this stunt, but I have to try. I have to see if Ryan still loves me the way I love him.

"I'm sorry, Carrie. I have to do this." I hang up before she has a chance to respond. I need a game plan, but I also need to do this by myself. My first reaction is to call Alex and have her by my side, but not this time. Yes, I'll call her, but I think I need to live in Boston for a while and get to know it the way Ryan does. I need to see if I can fall in love with this city like he has. I need to show him that he's the most important part of my life and that my career can wait.

chapter

six

When you break up with the one you love, your life changes. Many don't realize it, but that's why you make such a drastic change. Next, it could be your clothes, where you live and maybe even the way you look. You would think a change of that magnitude would mean the end of us. I certainly did and yet here I am, sitting in my designated game day seat waiting for my current girlfriend to join me while I'm thinking about my ex.

By all accounts, our break-up wasn't messy. She was out of town and I had already started working in Boston. It was a phone call from me, telling her that we needed time and space; that I didn't think we were working anymore. She was quiet, reserved and told me that she loved me. I replied in kind because I do love her. I have since I was seventeen, there's no mistaking that, but love can't save everything. I thought I'd hear from her and when I didn't, I picked up the phone to text

or call her only to find that I had nothing to say. When you get to that point in your life, it's best to step away.

Everything in me is telling me to ignore Hadley and her impromptu visit, but my heart won't let me. I'll never deny that we have a connection, but sometimes in life a connection isn't enough. Do I feel as strongly for Jessica as I do Hadley? No, I don't and I'm not sure I ever will, but that doesn't mean I should be with Hadley. Neither of us is willing to compromise and if you don't have at least that, you can't make your relationship work.

Jessica passes in front of me, bringing my attention to the here and now. She sits down and folds her hands in her lap, taking a deep breath. How she was able to so calmly walk out of my office today when Hadley arrived, I'll never understand. I want to ask her, but don't want to bring the subject up unless she's willing. Avoidance is going to be my forté until my life is back on track and Hadley is gone. I have a feeling she'll only be here a week, two tops. She can't stay away from New York, Alex and her music. I highly doubt Hadley is relocating her life to Boston just because I'm here.

I reach over and pull Jessica's hand into mine. We're not a PDA couple, but I think tonight calls for it. She needs to know that I'm still here and with her, despite what happened earlier.

Jessica smiles warmly, and it reminds me what a great person she is. She's probably the most down to earth person I know. She's unaffected by her social class, who her father is and the fact that she has some of the most prominent baseball players in her family home for dinners. In some ways, she and Hadley are a lot alike. That's probably why I'm attracted to her. Maybe she's my Boston version of Hadley because I couldn't have the real thing. No, that's not what she is at all. When I look at her, I see calm and peace, not the hectic lifestyle that I had before.

"Everything okay?" she asks. I want to tell her yes, that everything is fine, but that's a lie. I don't know what Hadley wants aside from being friends, and honestly that answer doesn't even suffice.

"I'm not sure, but I hope so."

Jessica squeezes my hand and offers me the most genuine smile. She's been down the path of dating someone famous, a high profile baseball player from another team. She quickly learned they weren't compatible but not before he pulled her into a nightmare public relations mess with his drug use and infidelity. She swore off anyone who's in the public eye, except for me. She knows how I feel about the media.

"What does she want?" The sad tone isn't falling on deaf ears. Jessica knows how I feel about Hadley. I've never hidden that fact. Love begins to fade over time and that's what Jessica has offered me – time. With each passing day, thoughts of Hadley ceased to exist. It's almost like she knew that I wasn't thinking about her any longer and had to show up. It's not that Jessica and I are taking the next step in our relationship and moving in with each other, but we're getting there. We're progressing at a nice, slow pace.

"I'm not sure, really. To be friends," I say, shrugging. Truth is I was in such a fog that I don't have a clue what Hadley's really doing here or if she's even still here. I hope she's on a plane back to New York. That would be classic Hadley fashion, a long distance relationship that works out over the phone.

"Are you going to see her again?" It's a valid question and one I wish I had the answer to. Hadley Carter is my weakness, my downfall. The fact that she's made an attempt to reach out proves that she's not over me. This wasn't some random 'on the street' meeting, but a full on attempt by her to reconnect. I'd love to say she won't be back, but I'd be lying, and I think we both know the truth.

"I don't know, Jessica." Her resolve slips, but her smile doesn't. No, she's not like that. She's a professional through and through. In this moment though, I want to take her out of the park and back to my apartment so we can figure this out, except I don't know what there is to figure out because I'm so freaking lost on what I should be doing. Do I run back to Hadley? Do I even give her another chance? Or do I tell her we're done and there's no hope for us? I have no doubt Jessica and Dylan would opt for the latter, but I'm not sure my heart can take it.

"Well I'm here for you, in whatever capacity you need me to be."

That right there is what makes Jessica stand out above every other woman I know. When I tell Dylan, she's going to flip and probably hunt Hadley down, but not Jessica. No, she offers me moral support even though another woman is in the picture. I don't deserve someone like her.

"I'm not going anywhere." I hate that I've said those words because I don't believe them and neither does she by the look in her eyes. I let go of her hand and place my arm on her shoulder, pulling her as close as she can get without hurting her on the armrest. I kiss her hair and hold my lips there as I fight the rage that's starting to build. I don't want to hurt Jessica and I don't want her to leave, but I want to know what the hell Hadley's up to.

chapter
seven

HADLEY

I want to be in the fairytale, the one where birds chirp when I wake telling me that today is going to be a good day. I want my Prince Charming to find me in the garden and profess his love to me. I want the happily ever after. I know it's silly to even think like that, but I can't help it. Love surrounds me every day and more so since I've been in Boston; whether it's the songs I'm writing or watching the people walk hand in hand, clearly in love, in Faneuil Hall. It's been three days since I ditched out on my tour and today it's in the headlines. "Hadley Carter Sidelined by Exhaustion." It's better than what I thought it would be: "Hadley Carter dumped by her Long-term Boyfriend for Baseball Royalty." I'm still not convinced that the truth won't come out and everyone will know I'm in Boston, where Ryan is openly public with his new girlfriend. My favorite ragtime, *TMZ*, will undoubtedly follow me around, and Ryan's life will be under the microscope. They live

to tear me down.

Today's the day that I work to get him back. I'm not sure how I'm going to do that, but it has to start today. I can't continue to sit by while his heart becomes lost to another. I'm not looking to cause problems, but love makes you do stupid things. He said we could be friends, and that's something we've never really been. For us, that's a good place to start. I just don't know what friends should do together, especially those that have been lovers. How am I going to make it through the day without touching him or resting my head on his shoulder? Neither of those will be easy, but I'm going to have to try.

Standing in front of my mirror with my hands down at my sides, I surmise that being in Boston is good for me. My skin looks clearer, and I have fewer bags under my eyes. The clothing style is different, more posh I guess you'd say. I've met some amazing people while I've toured the city and have found that I love a true Boston accent. I'm not trying to hide who I am here; there's no need. After today, every fan will know that I've taken up residence here, at least for the time being, and I'm not going to shy away from them. Although, from what I'm being told from locals, they don't give a 'pissah' who you are. They're already making me feel at home.

The soft knock on the door to my hotel room sends my heart into a frenzy. With one last look, I put on my happy face knowing that today's the fresh start we need, even if Ryan doesn't think we do.

I open the door quickly, hoping that I don't come off too eager. "Hi," I say breathlessly, as if I've run up a few flights of stairs to get to him. I feel that way now that he's standing in front of me with a dark polo shirt on, the sleeves rolled a few times to accentuate his biceps. Thinking back over the years from when I first met him, his transformation into a man has been a sight to behold. Most of it happened after we broke up the first time, but watching him keep up his physique has been a definite perk of being with him, a perk that I've missed and didn't realize how much until right now.

"Do you want to come in?" I move aside, pulling the door open, but he stands there with his hands in his pockets.

My lips go into a thin line at the realization that he probably doesn't want to be here. He's just appeasing me. I'm going to have to work a lot harder than I thought at winning him back if he's even available to be won. He may be done with me, and if that's the case, I don't blame him.

"I'll just get my stuff," I say, without making eye contact. I don't want him to be any more uncomfortable than he already is. I stall briefly, before picking up my bag and sunglasses. When I turn, he's still standing there like a statue. The better part of me wants to call off this date, but I have to try and see if he still feels the same way about me that I do him. One date, it's all I'm asking for.

"Are you ready?" He nods and sticks out his arm for me to take, just like he used to when we were together. The familiarity isn't lost on me, and I know better than to let the hope soar. This is going to be hard. I don't want him to do anything that compromises who he is or his job, but I'll be damned if I'm not taking his proffered arm.

We ride the elevator in silence. A few other hotel guests step on, take one look and start messing around on their phones. One can assume they're looking me up to confirm what they're minds are telling them. By the time they figure it out, hopefully we'll be out of this metal box and on our way. No one really chases you down unless they're looking for some dirty secrets.

"This is different," he says, as soon as we walk around the corner from the elevator exit. Light bulbs flash and questions are thrown at us. "Who was the woman you were with last night, Ryan?" "Is he cheating on you, Hadley?" "When did you call off your engagement?"

The last question causes me to falter in my steps, but Ryan keeps us walking. We've experienced this type of paparazzi onslaught when we first got together and shortly after my uncle Ian leaked a story about me chasing Ryan while he was still a minor. Bumps in the road, he called them. Except now we're in a ditch, and we'll need a ladder to get out.

As soon as we're outside, he's opening his car door for me. *His car door.* I run my hand over the soft leather and close my

eyes to will away the tears of a milestone I missed. I look out the front window the moment he slides in next to me.

"What's wrong?" he asks, immediately.

"Nothing."

"Don't lie to me, Hadley." He turns my chin so that I'm facing him. His eyes, the ones I fell so deeply in love with, are greener today than blue. I learned over the years that the color often changed depending on his mood or his clothing. Today, I'm not sure which is making the change for him. The thing about Ryan is that he can read me like an open book. I should be thankful, except I'm trying to keep my emotions in check. I'm hurt, angry and stupid, and I feel like I'm chasing after someone who is standing still just out of my grasp with each step I take.

"You bought a car, and I wasn't here to see it. I feel incredibly lost and stupid right now," I blurt out and watch his eyes widen at my mini tirade.

He leans back in his seat and shakes his head. "I didn't buy this car. I rented it for the day so you didn't have to walk." He runs his hand through his hair before looking at me. "I'm lost too, Hadley. Since you showed up, I'm not sure what to think anymore. My head is spinning, and my thoughts are racing a mile a minute, but you're far from stupid." He leans forward, his lips puckered. My body sighs when his lips press against my forehead. He doesn't pull away at first, and I take that as a sign.

"I wouldn't mind walking," I put that out there, letting him know that I'm going to be as flexible as I can be.

"Where I want to take you is pretty far." He pulls away and starts the car. When he pulls out into traffic I look behind to see if any of the paparazzi are following us. Thing is, I wouldn't know. We sat long enough in the car to give them an opportunity to. I just hope they don't rain on my parade. I just want one day.

chapter
eight

RYAN

I want to kick my own ass. For days, I've been avoiding Hadley, and everything seemed to be working in my favor. Phone calls went unreturned, and text messages were replied with only a word or two. I wasn't going to give her any room to weasel her way back into my life. A life, mind you, that I'm trying to rebuild. A life in which, I have a girlfriend.

My girlfriend, Jessica, is a sweet, beautiful and completely understanding woman, and she showed up at my apartment last night looking so forlorn. Letting her in was a mistake. Not because I don't love her but because of what she said and did. When she sat down, she opened her bag and poured almost every magazine cover featuring Hadley and me on my coffee table. I sat across from her, looking at the stockpile wondering what in the hell she was thinking. When she explained to me that for the past few days she has been researching us, against her better judgment, she came to the conclusion that

Hadley and I have unresolved feelings that need to be taken care of before Jessica and I can move on to the next step in our relationship. I balked. She walked out, leaving all the magazines lying haphazardly in front of me, reminding me of a past I'm finding hard to forget.

Pure torture. I caved, and now here I am in the seat of a rental car driving my ex fiancée, who is still wearing my ring, to Cape Cod. When I texted Hadley, asking her if she wanted to spend the day with me, I hadn't a clue what to do. To say I feel both awkward and relieved makes me feel like I'm a walking contradiction. I love Hadley and seven or eight months ago I would've welcomed her back with open arms. But when you start giving your heart to another person who deserves to be loved, it's hard to just shut yourself off.

I decided on one of the most sought-after vacation spots in New England, knowing that she wants me back, and I'm here because my current girlfriend thinks this is a good idea. If I ever hear a woman say men are confusing, I'm going to sit her down and tell her my story.

Waking up this morning, I thought this would be a piece of cake. I'd show up, take her out and go back to ignoring her. Jessica would be happy. Hadley would leave. I'd go back to my daily business. Except she opened the door, and I saw the real Hadley staring back at me, not the pop princess that everyone loves and worships. I saw the sweet, loving, beautiful woman that I fell in love with, twice in my life, giving me her biggest smile. I also saw that smile fall when I refused to cross the threshold of her hotel room. Yet I didn't hesitate to offer her my arm, and that's why I want to kick my own ass.

Sitting beside her now, I have my hand under my leg as I drive across the Bourne Bridge. I glance over at her every so often and watch her as she takes in the sights. She lets out little squeals of delight when something catches her eye, and with each one I want to pull my hand out from under my leg and touch her. I want to feel her skin against my fingertips because I've missed her. Had I not offered her my arm back at the hotel, I don't think I would feel this way… maybe.

"Oh Ryan, the air…" she has her window rolled down and

her eyes are closed. It's in this moment that I realize what town I need to take her to.

"It's a lot different than New York," I put out there. I wanted her to move with me, but she was never keen on the idea. Not that I want her to now, but I want her to love this area as much as I do. I want her to see that she was wrong and that we could've made a life here. She doesn't reply, and I know I struck a nerve with her. It wasn't my intention, but I'm pleased with myself for doing so.

I pull into the parking lot and watch in amazement as her eyes light up. Waves are crashing against the rocks. Kites are flying high in the sky, and there are yachts and sail boats, visible from where we're parked, floating out in the ocean. I was smart enough to think ahead and brought a blanket, just in case. Until I pulled in here, I wasn't sure what we were going to do today. After getting out of the car and grabbing the blanket, I open her door for her. She takes my hand, but as soon as she's standing, I let go. The hurt on her face doesn't escape my notice and the ache in my heart grows. I'm not a free man though, and she has to understand that.

We walk side by side and trudge through the sand until we decide on a spot to sit. It's peaceful out here and I thought about moving to the Cape, but with my job being mostly in the summer and the traffic, I thought better of it.

As soon as we're sitting, her sandals are off and her toes are digging into the sand. I laugh as she wiggles her red-polished toes free, only to push them under again.

"Do you know how long it's been since I've been to the beach?"

I shake my head. "Unless you went without me…" I shrug, not sure how to finish my train of thought. It pains me to think of Hadley with someone else, but I can't fault her if she was. Doing so makes me a hypocrite.

"Years, Ryan. The last time was with you."

I pull my legs up and rest my arms on top of my knees. I take a deep breath and prepare myself for what I'm about to say. "Hadley, you asked me when I was seventeen where my dream date would be, beach or home, and I said beach." I

shake my head and refuse to look at her. "I shouldn't be here because I'm with Jessica, but I am, and this is something we should've done a long time ago. Ending our relationship the way we did was wrong. We owed it to ourselves to be better for each other, stronger."

"I know," she whispers.

"We're both at fault for the demise of our relationship, and something tells me that you're not accepting that we're over."

She shakes her head and looks at me. "That's not it, Ryan. I didn't take off my ring not because I didn't want to accept we were through, but out of respect for you and your new job. I didn't want the media all over you, and I didn't want it to spotlight the tour. I know I'm a selfish person. I know I don't deserve to be here right now. We used to make sense and then one day we didn't. I think for a bit we wanted different things, and now we're here. As much as I'd love to think we're on the same page, I know we're not."

She's right. We weren't.

"I think our lives would be so different if we had stayed together when I was seventeen."

She nods. "I know they would be, but you wouldn't be happy. We needed that break. You had to grow and I really needed to find myself. I just hated that we lost each other in the mix." Hadley mimics my position, but lays her head on her arms and looks at me. "Do you regret us?"

I shake my head slowly so she can see me. "Never. I love you, Hadley. I think I always will."

"Where did we go wrong?"

I let out a deep breath and laugh. "Well, the list is long." I slip off my shoes and bury my toes in the sand. The gritty feeling is a true statement of how my heart feels right now. You either love it or hate it, and right now I'm not sure which I prefer. "I wanted get married and travel. You wanted kids and wanted me to raise them while you toured. I didn't have the best life growing up, but I do know I want to raise my children with my wife in a home with stability."

She nods. "Alex and Cole have a baby," she says softly. "A little girl."

"So does Dylan," I add. "I'm going to be honest with you because I feel that you deserve at least that from me. Holding Dylan's daughter, it changed my perspective. I want a family, Hadley, but not at the expense where my children are growing up without a mother around all the time."

"Am I too late?" she asks, her voice breaking.

I swallow hard and stare out into the wide-open space before us. "I can't answer that right now."

chapter
nine

I'm back to day one and standing outside the giant stadium. I know I'm taking a risk by coming here again, but after yesterday I can't stop thinking about what Ryan said. He poured out his heart, leaving me somewhat blindsided, but also with the hope that there might be a chance. I'm the epitome of evil though, trying to steal another woman's man. A situation like this is what makes great songs. I'm a stupid cliché and my own worst enemy. The last thing I want is for Ryan to hate me so I'm taking the hands-off approach. If Ryan reaches out for my hand, I'm going to nicely reject him. I don't want the paparazzi to snap an innocent picture and blast it all over *Page Six* with a bogus headline. That's not fair to Ryan or his girlfriend, and out of respect for her I'm going to do my best to keep Ryan faithful.

I'm not, however, giving up. I can't. He opened a window for me yesterday, and that tells me that he's not in love with

Jessica. When he told me that he still loved me, my heart did a little shimmy, but I'm not naïve enough to think it's the same type of love we've shared or what he's feeling now for Jessica.

I have to remind myself to say her name. To make sure she has an identity in all of this. The minute I forget I know I'll do something stupid. It's not just Ryan and I; there are three of us in this triangle that I've created. Thing is, even if I knew about Jessica I'd still be here trying my hardest to get Ryan back. He's my soul mate, my partner. I'm not nearly the person I should be without him. Ryan Stone completes me in every way possible. I've known that for almost ten years now.

Walking down the corridor, this time without my heels to make my presence known, I take the same escalator as I did before. The receptionist is at her desk this time and looks up when the door opens. I give her my best Hadley Carter smile and am graciously rewarded with one in return.

"May I help you?"

"I'm here to see Ryan Stone."

"Do you have an appointment?"

I should have a standing one, but I ruined any chance of that happening. I shake my head quickly, much to her disdain. I catch the slight eye roll she's performing before she looks away.

"Let me see if he's free." She looks down at her desk briefly before turning to her computer. "Mr. Stone is on a conference call. It could be awhile."

"I'll wait," I say with a sugary tone. She doesn't like me, I can tell. For all I know she could be best friends with Jessica, who could walk in any minute and go right into his office, but I can't. I'm the outsider, the home wrecker. I pick up a copy of *Live Entertainment* and blanch. Of course Ryan and I are on the cover. The headline is nothing glamorous.

Renegades General Manager, Ryan Stone, seems to be playing the 'field' as he's seen with his former girlfriend, pop sensation, Hadley Carter.

I'm tempted to read the article, but know it will be nothing

but this source said this and that when in fact there are no sources. Alex doesn't know what's going on, as I've dodged all her calls. Carrie would never speak to the press unless we were issuing a statement, and since I never comment on my public life, that's never happening. That does leave Dylan. She'd yap until she's blue in the face if it paints me in a bad light and of course, Jessica. She could be heartbroken and wallowing at home for all I know, except she's probably not because she still has Ryan. I shuffle through the other magazines, but they're mostly about baseball. A topic that I should know about, but don't. Truth is, I never took an interest in Ryan's job and for that I'm kicking myself. It's not that I didn't care, but I've never been a sports fan.

"Hadley?"

I look up to find a surprised Ryan standing in front of me. He's in a suit and looking so sophisticated. I stand and greet him with a kiss on each cheek.

"How long have you been out here?"

I look at my watch quickly before seeking out his eyes. "About twenty minutes. It's okay. I know you're busy, and I'm probably interrupting your day.

He turns his head and glances at the receptionist who quickly turns her back to him. "Come in to my office."

The child in me wants to stick my tongue out at her, but I refrain. I *really* don't need that headline in tomorrow's gossip column. I follow Ryan into his office and again marvel at the size of the windows that afford him a view of the ballpark. I'm instantly drawn to the action outside and stand there, looking out.

"Want a tour?" I feel Ryan step behind me. He's close enough that I can smell his cologne. The scents of sandalwood and peppermint with a hint of citrus send my hormones into overdrive. If we were in another place, another time, I'd be in his arms.

"I'd like that very much," I say, turning toward him. There are only inches between us. Our hands brush against each other, and I feel his fingers repeat the grazing motion. His eyes are focused on mine so intently. His head turns slightly and I

follow.

"Ryan, I…" the voice and clearing of a throat causes him to step back. "I'm sorry, I didn't mean to interrupt."

"You didn't, Jessica. I was just asking Hadley if she wanted a tour."

I smile at Jessica, but turn away. I don't want to see her staring at Ryan. I don't want to see hurt in her eyes because of what she just witnessed. Had Ryan kissed me in that moment, I would've allowed it because I'm that selfish.

I can see their silhouettes reflected through the windows, and instead of watching the guys on the field I'm watching them. His hand rests on her hip and their backs are to me. The hushed tones bother me, but this is his office. I'm sure it's business and not personal. I would hope she's not over there planning my demise, although if I were in her shoes that's exactly what I'd be doing.

When I see Ryan turn toward me, I avert my eyes and pretend I'm capitated by the man swinging the bat.

"Are you ready?"

I turn and offer him a smile. He doesn't smile back, but I don't let that ruin this moment. He places his hand on the small of my back and leads me out of his office.

"Why are there so many people now? These halls were empty when I arrived."

"It's game day. We have a lot of seasonal employees here, and most show up two to three hours before the gates open."

I stop in my tracks. "Oh Ryan, I wasn't aware. I'm sorry. I can come back."

"Don't be silly," he says as he pushes us along. We take the escalator down and stop in front of the souvenir stand. "What's your pleasure, Ms. Carter?"

"Excuse me?"

Ryan laughs. "Well, I figured since you're here and it's game day, we'd catch a game."

"I've never been to a game."

"I know, Hadley, and we're about to change that."

After I pick out a hat and a t-shirt, Ryan and I go to dinner and by dinner I mean we walk a few feet and order hotdogs,

nachos, popcorn and a giant pretzel to share. He said we'd share, but I'm a bit skeptical. With our food in our hands, he leads us to our seats. I hear the whispers as I descend the steps, but ignore them. I'm here to watch a baseball game with the man of my dreams, and if that means no autographs tonight, I'm going to do just that.

Ryan and I sit down and my hand instantly delves into the popcorn. "God this stuff is so bad for us."

"I know, but it's a staple. You *have* to get popcorn and a hotdog at a baseball game."

I nod as I bite into mine. "This is really good."

He laughs as he eats his. "Everything that's bad for you is good."

"Excuse me." We both look up to find five or six girls standing off to the side of us. "Can we get a picture?"

I look at Ryan and don't miss the eye roll. I clear my throat. "Not tonight. I'm sorry." I've never seen faces fall so fast, but I want to be a normal person tonight with Ryan. As soon as they're gone, he smiles. I bump his shoulder with mine, and he laughs again.

After we stand for the National Anthem, the game gets underway. Ryan is the perfect host in explaining everything to me. Deep into the eighth inning, the game is tied and we're up to bat. I'm leaning forward with my hands clasped, praying like everyone else in the park for a hit. The batter swings and we can all hear the ball hit the bat. Heads all move in slow motion as we follow the ball as it flies out of the park. The stadium erupts in cheers as we all stand up.

"Oh my God, Ryan, did you see that?" I ask as I clutch his arm. I'm so excited I miss the chance to give him a high five. Once our hands connect, everything around us stops. Ryan leans toward me as I wet my lips. As much as I should shy away, I can't. I love him too much to deny myself a chance.

Our lips touch, briefly, and I jump as fireworks go off behind us. He straightens, but keeps his eyes on me.

"Maybe I can see you tomorrow?"

"I'd love that," I reply, nodding my agreement.

chapter
ten

I look at the clock above my mantle and watch the second hand tick by. The time is moving painstakingly slow, and with each minute that passes, my anxiety increases. I was so stupid last night, kissing Hadley like that, but can't deny that it felt amazing. I pulled away as soon as I registered what I was doing, but the damage had already been done. Jessica could've very well seen us from her father's box seats, and hurting Jessica is the very last thing I want to do. However, hurting Hadley isn't an option either.

When I left New York, I thought I left her behind. I never imagined she'd show up here, especially not a year later. The feelings I had, they're still there and stronger than ever. The old adage, absence makes your heart grows fonder, is exact in my case. Hadley and I needed a year apart from each other to grow. The issue with that is the only way to grow is to see other people. I happened to meet an amazing woman who

listened to me whine about my failed relationship. Jessica and I connected over our love of sports, particularly baseball, and our failures at high-profile relationships.

Now I'm sitting here waiting for Jessica so I can confess my sins and ask for forgiveness. We'll break up because it's the right thing to do. I can't lead her and Hadley on, and if I'm having trouble fighting my feelings for Hadley – who no doubt knows what's going to happen the next time I'm with her – I don't want to do cheat on Jessica. It's not fair to her, and she's been a trooper through all of this. I owe her the respect she's earned by being honest.

The sound of Jessica's key sliding into the door makes my heart thrash a rapid pace. I should stand and greet her, but I feel as if I have cinderblocks holding me down. I quickly turn on the television and act as if I didn't hear her come in. When she enters my living room, she leans up against the wall. She's dressed to go running, which means she's not planning on staying.

"Hey," I say, stupidly. She smiles softly, but it doesn't reach her eyes. "Come sit down." I adjust so that I'm open to her with my leg under my other one. She sits and reaches for my hand. Our fingers intertwine, and I look for my body to respond the same way it does with Hadley. I shake my head lightly when I don't have the desired results.

"I saw you," she says in a hushed tone. I nod, confirming that, yes, I screwed up.

"I'm sorry, Jessica."

"You don't have to be sorry, Ryan. I told you to see her. I have no one to blame but myself."

I pull her to me and hold her in my arms. I don't know why I can't be in love with her so deeply that she's the only one I see. She's perfect for me and maybe that's the problem. Maybe I don't need perfect. I need crazy and wild. I need the opposite of who I am to keep me grounded.

Jessica pulls away, but stays close to me. "I didn't want to watch you, but as soon as I saw her turn those fans away I knew she was changing for you."

I nod because after watching Hadley do that, knowing

what it could cost her, it showed me that she's willing to make us work. "It's not as simple as turning away some fans though. You know that my problems with her stem from her tours. She was always gone, and that's not what I want out of life."

"I know, but I also know you have a connection. You've been good to me, Ryan, the best, in some cases. You're sweet, personable and very good-looking, but your heart belongs to another."

I blush at her compliments and chide myself at same time. I don't deserve them. "My heart belongs to you too and I don't know what to do."

"Ah, sounds like you're in a pickle."

I laugh hard at her baseball terminology, but she's right. I have Jessica on one base and Hadley on another with me running in between them not sure which way I should go. The funny part, one would choose the safest route, and that would be Jessica, not Hadley.

I pick up her hand and hold it mine. "I don't want to hurt you, Jessica. It's the last thing I want to do, but I'm really off kilter here. I didn't mean to kiss Hadley last night, but I also wouldn't take it back."

"I know, Ryan. I'm not blaming you. I knew when I told you to give her a chance that this could be the outcome. I'm not stupid, but I'm also not willing to be someone's second best. With you, I was guaranteed to be second whether you thought that way or not. From the first day we met, you found a way to slip Hadley into the conversation. I don't know if you were doing it subconsciously or what, but I never questioned your devotion to her."

"She's all I've known."

"I know, and maybe you guys needed a year apart to figure out your lives. If I do remember correctly, she started performing at a young age and spent her teen years in a tour bus. She probably missed a lot of that growing up part."

I nod because it's true. Ian had her touring so much that she missed everything. Eventually, she started dating Cole until he cheated on her. She went through a very public break-up with him that caused a lot of untrue and very nasty rumors

to surface.

"I'm going to make a decision for you, Ryan, because honestly I don't think you know what you want. I'm going to break things off. If you can't work things out with Hadley, give me a call. I know all your baggage and while my feelings may be hurt, when I commit to a man, I need to be his number one."

Jessica stands, leaving me stunned by her words. Somehow I'm able to rise to my feet and walk her to the door. She sets my key, which is already off her keychain, on the hall table. She was going to break up with me today, regardless.

I pull her into my arms before she steps out into the hallway. "I'm sorry, Jessica."

"I know, Ryan."

I cup her face gently and place my lips to hers. The spark I thought I had with her is no longer there, and only images of Hadley flash behind my closed eyelids.

"Bye, Jessica." She nods, but doesn't say anything as she closes the door. I lean against the wall and slide down, holding my head in my hands. One would think I have a clear path to pursue Hadley, but I don't. I'm not convinced that Hadley and I should be together or if we'll even work. There are things that I want and need from her and vice versa.

I know we're going to have to compromise, and for me it will mostly revolve around her touring. If we're going to be together, things have to change. I won't go back to how things were and New York isn't an option.

I stand and walk over to my window, looking out over the street. It's lined with cars; people are home for the weekend. There has to be something downtown that we can visit and be tourists together. I pull out my phone and call Hadley.

"Hey."

"Want to be a tourist today?"

She giggles. "I am a tourist right now."

"Meet me downtown in fifteen minutes. We're going to go on the duck boat." I don't give her a chance to respond before hanging up. If we're going to work, I need her to love Boston as much as I do.

chapter
eleven

HADLEY

Today should be one of the happiest days of my life. It's a slight exaggeration but it's supposed to be important, nonetheless. When Ryan called and asked me to be a tourist, I had far greater expectations than sitting in a public restroom puking my guts out. Who knew I got seasick? Definitely not Ryan or he wouldn't have suggested this godforsaken duck tour.

We kissed the other night at the ballgame, but I'm not sure he meant to. Call it the heat of the moment, in the action and whatnot. His demeanor toward me has been lukewarm at best, and I know he's just simply appeasing me until I decide to return to New York or restart my tour. He knows me too well.

I rinse my mouth with the tepid water from the faucet and drag myself out of the restroom. Ryan is standing against a tree, his legs crossed at his ankles and he's looking at his phone. I've told myself that I can't be jealous of his girlfriend.

I put him in that situation, and it's something I have to accept. I'm just incredibly thankful that he wants to spend time with me. I don't deserve it.

My steps are staggered, and I feel like I've been run over by a diesel truck minus the tire treads. Ryan looks up and pockets his phone, his smile bright and welcoming. I wish that alone were enough to ease my stomach.

"Are you feeling okay? You look a little green."

I shake my head but have to stop and close my eyes to keep my equilibrium intact. "As much as I want to be here, Ryan, I need to go back to my hotel."

"Okay, let's get a cab." Ryan places his arm around me, and I mold to his side, resting my head between his shoulder and chest. I've missed this and hate knowing he's only doing it because I'm sick. Once we're inside, he pulls me to him. I'm fighting the hope that's building that this means more than it does, but my heart is screaming at me to accept it, to run with it. Sadly, if I did that I'd probably get five steps away before he cuts me off or reminds me that he has a girlfriend.

I close my eyes for the duration of the cab ride. The stop-and-go motion isn't helping my queasiness at all. The driver comes to a screeching halt making me so thankful that we're out of this metal contraption. Now only an elevator ride and I'm home free.

"I'll pay you back for the cab ride," I mumble as we walk through the lobby. It hasn't escaped my notice that the paparazzi haven't been around today. Maybe someone more famous is in town, garnering all their attention. Whatever it may be, I'm thankful that I'm not being caught looking the way I do.

Ryan rifles through my purse to find my hotel key while I stand against the wall with my hands on my knees, bent at the waist. To say I'm pissed at myself would be an understatement. He calls to take me out and this happens. I know our days together are probably few and far between, and I need to make the most of the days that he's offering. Today was a total fail.

"Let's get you into bed." Ryan picks me up and cradles me to his chest, kicking the door shut behind us. Any other time,

I'd say this is romantic. I'm just grateful that I don't have to walk.

"I need some water."

"I'll get it for you, don't worry. I won't leave you." I pretend that his words aren't phasing me, but the truth is that my heart is now beating so fast I'm sure he can hear it. He sets me down gently on the bed and quickly works to remove my shoes.

"Where are your pajamas?"

"In the bathroom, I'll get them," I say, attempting to stand. I have to hang onto the bed, but I'm determined to make it there before him.

"I'll do it, Hadley, just lie down." Ryan sidesteps me and beats me to the bathroom. I accept the inevitable and sit down. When he comes out, he's holding his t-shirt and boxers. I try to smile, but it turns more into a smirk.

"I missed you; they made me feel close to you." I shrug. Ryan's grin is small, but I see it. I try not to see too much in that smile and just relish in the fact that he's here, helping me out. He could've bailed by now.

"Um… I'll just let you change."

I nod, remembering the last time I was sick he did everything for me. We even soaked in our garden tub until the water ran cold. Not this time though. I sigh when the bedroom door clicks leaving me surrounded by silence. I hate the quiet. I change as quickly as my body allows me to move. I'm feeling better than I was, but still very queasy.

Ryan knocks just as I slip his t-shirt over my head. "Come in."

The door opens and Ryan steps in with a tray of food. I look at him questioningly. "Where did you get that?"

"Room service."

"I'm aware of that, but they're never this fast."

"I ordered it online. It's just soup and some toast, nothing much until we know you can keep it down," he says, walking over to my nightstand and positioning the tray so it doesn't fall. "In you go." Ryan pulls back my comforter and holds out his hand.

Reluctantly, I put my hand in his, but stall. "This is not how

I wanted our day to be," I say with nothing but melancholy in my voice. This is absolutely the worst date ever. Ryan arranges my pillows so I can sit up and tucks the blankets in around me. He's acting like a father. I suppose that's all I'm going to get because I don't deserve any more.

Ryan sits next to me and hands me my cup of soup. I don't want to do this with him. Not like this.

"You can go, Ryan. I can manage. I've been doing it for a year now." The second the words are out of my mouth I'm looking away. I chance a look at him and see indifference.

"You can't do this alone, and that's not why I'm here."

"Yes, I can," I stick out my chin in defiance.

"No, you can't," he says, turning to face me. "For the past five years I've been there and when I wasn't, you had Alex. I'm not saying it's a bad thing, but when you think about it, you don't do anything by yourself."

I roll my eyes. "That's not true. I went sightseeing the other day."

"That's good. You should get out and see Boston. I love it here, and I'd love it…" Ryan shakes his head.

"What were you going to say?"

"Nothing. Please eat." He motions to the soup sitting in front of me. As much as I don't want to, I take a sip and let the warm broth cure my ailment. Ryan sits on the edge of my bed, his arms resting on his knees. I hate that he's not looking at me, but I did that. Once again, I've screwed things up.

"I'm sorry, Ryan."

Ryan sits up and rubs his hands on his shorts. "Don't be sorry for something you meant. We broke up, Hadley, and now here we are. Things are awkward and feelings are in the way. We left a lot of stuff unsaid and if we want to get past this, we need to talk it out." Ryan stands, walking over to the wall and leaning against it.

"I love you, Hadley. I have for a long time, but when you put your career in front of us, something had to give. I know you can probably say the same thing about me, but I refuse to be a kept man. I don't like the way it feels. I want to work and provide a home. I don't want a wife who is doing it all while I

sit around and watch TV. That's not me.

"I asked you to marry me and every time a date was set, it changed because of a tour or a new album. It was always something, and I couldn't live like that. I *can't* live like that. I accepted your job from day one, that's never been a problem. What I can't accept is a wife who is never home, who goes on year-long tours and expects to raise children on a tour bus."

Tears fall as Ryan finishes telling me everything that he wants. There's nothing to dispute; he's right about everything. I just didn't know he was right until it was too late. It took the birth of Alex and Cole's daughter to open my eyes. Seeing my best friend with her baby really made me stop and think.

Ryan clears his throat. "I know I said I didn't want children right now, but since Dylan had her daughter, I think I've changed my mind. No, I know I have, but I can't do that with you unless you're willing to stop touring so much. It's the tours that kill me, Hadley, not the music. Not the paparazzi or your recording schedule. It's the tours that take eight months or over a year. You're Hadley Carter, America's Pop Princess – give America a break and stay home, enjoy life. No one is going to fault you for wanting to settle down. They'll all still be there."

"I understand," I mumble through my tears. Ryan steps forward and kisses my forehead.

"I'll call you tomorrow."

With that, he walks out of my room. I sob the moment the door to my hotel room shuts because I'm not so sure he'll call tomorrow or if I'll ever see him again.

chapter
twelve

RYAN

It's been two days since I last saw Hadley. I didn't call her like I said I would. I couldn't bring myself to. It's not that I didn't want to talk to her or even see her, I just couldn't do it. When I left her in her hotel room, I heard her break down and it took everything in me to keep walking. Had I gone back, I would've most likely done something I'm not ready for or sent her the wrong message. As much as I love her, I'm not sure being together is the answer. It would be too easy to fall back into the same pattern. I have no doubt the initial return of us would be explosive and sensational, but what happens when the newness wears off and we're back to facing the same issues? What happens if she doesn't like Boston as much as I do and is adamant we return to New York, or worse, we end up divorced because of it? I can't have that. When I marry, I want it to be until death do us part. I know the statistics on celebrity marriages, and they don't bode well.

My phone mocks me, and I find myself looking at it every few minutes. My hand twitches as if it knows I want to call her, but I can't. The pile of contracts in front of me that need to be reviewed can and will take me all day. I need to focus on my job and not whether or not I'm going to rekindle my love affair with Hadley Carter.

I rub my hands over my face, groaning with each pass over.

"Tough day?"

I look up to find Jessica standing in my doorway, her arm full of folders. "Hey you," I say, hoping that she and I are on the good side of things. She walks in and sits in front of my desk. A week ago, she would've walked over to where I'm sitting, but things have changed. I take her in, study her for a moment. She doesn't look upset or even angry with me.

"I'm good, Ryan."

"That's good," I reply as I lean back in my chair. "I'm really -"

She holds up her hand to stop me. "You don't have to say you're sorry. I've known for a while that you still loved her. It's hard to forget that first love, the one that is so powerful it consumes you fully. Someday I hope to have those feelings for someone, and I think you're both incredibly lucky to have found each other."

My lips press into a thin line as I shake my head. This woman, the one in front of me, is beyond amazing. I wish I had met her at a different time in my life. Thing is though, I've only known Hadley.

"You're amazing," I tell her with a small head shake. "I don't know how I ever got so lucky with you, but someone is going to be very, very lucky to have you, and I'm sorry. If I had thought that Hadley would come back the way she did, I would've never started anything with you. The last thing I want to do is hurt you."

Jessica leans forward reaching for my hand. I give it to her willingly. "I'm not hurt, Ryan. A little sad, yes, but I consider you my friend, and we had a great time together."

I smile. "We did, didn't we?"

"Boss, I need help." Jessica and I break apart when my star

third basemen, Ethan Davenport, walks in. Ethan was a top a recruit out of college. Every major team wanted him whether they had a third baseman or not. The Renegades were lucky. We had the room to pay him, meet his contract needs and desperately needed him on the field. The problem with Ethan is, he's twenty-one, six-foot-two with light blue eyes and dark hair, a little bit crazy and has a gaggle of women hounding him on a nightly basis. Of course, he told social media where his apartment is, so that's not helping. He's Boston's most eligible bachelor and loves playing that role. Right now he's pulling on his hair, which is a telltale sign that he's agitated. I learned that this last year when I was recruiting him.

"I'll see you guys later. Ryan, don't forget we have a three o'clock."

"I'll be there." I watch her walk-out and wait for the pain of not having her in my life to set in. When it doesn't, it only tells me what I already know. "Have a seat, Ethan."

Ethan sits in the chair that Jessica just left. His leg starts bouncing immediately and his eyes dart all over the room. If I didn't know better, I'd think he was on drugs, but he's not. He's the poster boy for clean health and even though he frequents the bars, he's never caught drinking. I don't know what he does behind closed doors, but at least in public he's not out embarrassing himself.

Sometimes it's hard for me to be the boss around here. Being the youngest GM in history, it puts me close to most of my players' ages. Some of them, not all, think that we're buddies. They forget that I call the shots and can trade them or not renew their contracts. It's a hard pill to swallow for these guys. At times, I'd love to be their buddy, but at the end of the day, I'm their boss and lines can't be crossed.

"What's going on?" I ask, ready to tackle whatever problem he has.

"Okay, so you know that Renegades blogger?"

I nod.

"Well he or she, I don't know who it is, but they keep writing about me."

I lean forward and clasp my hands together. "They're

allowed. You're a public figure, playing a public game and its freedom of speech. I've seen the blog; there's nothing derogatory being posted."

"Boss, they post about when I pick my nose. Not about my stats or anything like that."

I stifle a laugh. "So, stop picking your nose, Ethan."

He rolls his eyes and fidgets with the arm rests. "I can't… I mean I can, but my hands have to be doing something while I'm waiting for the ball."

When we acquired Ethan, I had him tested for a tic disorder, nerve damage, anything the doctors could think of and everything came back normal. This kid can't sit still, no matter how hard he tries.

"Listen, you've done a great job keeping your head in the game. So what if this person blogs about your on-field antics. My suggestion is to stop reading the blog and stop looking up your name online because if it's not this blog, it's going to be the next one that has something to say. Read ESPN. They're accurate and have all your stats updated."

"Am I interrupting?"

My head springs at the sound of Hadley's voice. Against my will, a smile spreads across my face when we lock eyes. Ethan turns in his seat and mutters, "whoa." I want to throw my pen at him, but resist.

"Come on in, we're just about finished."

Ethan turns back around and leans forward. "Boss, that's Hadley Carter!" he all but screams when he says her name.

"I know who she is, Ethan."

"But how…?" he begs for an answer.

Hadley sits down next to him and his leg stops bouncing. He stares at her, much like the women stare at him. I'm staring too though because she's rocking a pair of cut-off shorts and a tank-top. Her long blond hair is pulled up into a high ponytail and her sunglasses are sitting on top of her head. Her skin is sun-kissed and looking so much better than it was the other day when we were together. If I didn't already have carnal knowledge of her body, I'd be on my hands and knees begging for her to give me an ounce of attention. I pull myself a little

closer to my desk to hide the issue developing in my slacks. One thing's for sure, Hadley knows how to push my buttons… all of my buttons.

Clearing my throat, more so to break my reverie so I can concentrate, I look at Ethan, who is still eyeing Hadley with a shit-eating grin on his face. "Hadley and I…" I stop because I'm not sure how to explain us without it coming out wrong.

"We were engaged once," she blurts out.

Ethan's head slowly turns and looks at me. I'm a statue, afraid of showing any emotion or confirmation. He shakes his head. "Man, boss, you're one lucky bastard." He gets up and leaves, shutting my door behind him.

"Well, that was interesting."

Hadley starts laughing, which warms my cold interior. I've missed her and I don't know why I keep fighting it. Life is supposed to be about following your dreams, taking risks and getting lost in love. I have my dream job. Hadley is definitely a risk. Getting lost in love with her is the easiest thing I've ever done.

"Come here," I say as I beckon her with my finger. She stands and walks over to me. I push my chair back and place my hands on her hips. I guide her to stand in between my legs and let my hands caress the back of her thighs. "You're dangerous for me, Hadley, but I can't stay away. I tried. I thought if I ignored you, you'd go away, and I could just push away these feelings, act like they don't exist, but I can't. With that said, it scares me that after a few months, I was able to move on, or try to move on. I don't want to feel like that."

"I don't either." Her fingers push through my hair, a feeling that I've missed.

"Will you move to Boston?"

She nods. "Yes, I will."

"Will you be my girlfriend? Can we date, be together and see where things lead us? I don't want to rush into anything."

"I'd really like that, Ryan."

I stand quickly and pull her to my lips. The sensation coursing through me is new, almost as if we've never kissed before. I have an uncontrolled storm rolling through my body

right now, and she's the umbrella that's going to keep me dry.

When I pull away, I rest my forehead against hers. She's breathing heavily, while I'm barely hanging on.

"Sorry, I just had to know," I whisper against her lips, unable to keep my lips off of her.

"Know what?"

"If you're still the one for me." My words linger in air as my smile grows wide, assuring her that yes, she is the one. The only one for me.

If her smile is any indication by how happy she is, I'd say she's on top of the moon... or charts in her case.

chapter
thirteen

HADLEY

It's been six months since I moved to Boston, and I have no regrets. The spring weather quickly turned humid and at times unbearable, but I managed to get through it with my trusty air conditioner. With fall approaching, I'm seeing more and more tourists flocking to all the right locations.

A favorite of mine is sitting on the park bench at Faneuil Hall and watching the street performers. A few times, I've brought my guitar and sang, but it's not too often that I can do that unless I set up some type of security.

The one thing I haven't grown accustomed to is a true Bostonian accent. The words they say often result in me staring bug-eyed at them and shaking my head. There's a group of them that sit behind Ryan and me at each ballgame. They get rowdy and sometimes throw their beers at unsuspecting Yankee fans. It's a love/hate relationship.

I've become a fan of the Renegades and while I'm still

learning the game, it's enjoyable to watch. Most importantly, it's giving Ryan and me some much needed time to be together. My tour will start in the spring once Ryan's back to work. We agreed that I'd tour while he's working, only one month overseas and nothing after the month of October. I owe it to my fans, the ones I cancelled on, to finish out the tour. The press hounded me for about two weeks into my stay in Boston and I finally came clean, appearing for the first time in years without my engagement ring.

Ryan and I opted to donate it to charity. He said if we're to travel the path of an engagement again, he'll get me something new, something that's not tainted with bitterness and anger. We still live in separate apartments, and I think that's something we needed. When we got back together six years ago, we started living together right away. No dating, no courting, just together and sharing everything. This time around, things are different, better. We talk more. We make plans to see each other. We surprise each other at work. We're more spontaneous and not acting like we've been married for years.

I'm back to writing music and recording almost daily, but only while Ryan's at work. I'm renting a small studio near the stadium, which allows us to go to lunch or leave from work and walk to dinner.

When I told Carrie that I was moving to Boston, she wasn't too happy, but she's dealing with the three hour drive that she makes twice a week. Alex and Cole, and their daughter Hayden moved to Connecticut, splitting the difference between Boston and NYC. Cole is back in the studio and has a number 1 hit on the radio. Dylan, she's another story, and I don't see her much. I know it hurts Ryan and that her and I don't get along, but there isn't anything I can do aside from leaving him and I won't do that. Dylan comes around when I'm not there, and it's something I've had to accept. I placate her with niceties and give her daughter presents, but that's the extent of our relationship. I have Alex, he has Dylan. We've learned to accept things the way they are.

Today, I'm watching a group of young boys street dance.

It's not the first time I've seen this particular group and have talked to Carrie about using them in a music video. The talent they have is unparalleled. They're not classically trained, and I think that's where they have an advantage. They choreograph their own steps and allow their bodies to move to the music. They're definitely my favorite type of street performer.

Just beyond their circle, there's a man playing drums on anything and everything – except a set of drums. He's the entertainment. He's the one providing the beat right now. He's also my inspiration for new music. Because of him I want to break out into something else, a sound more edgy and less auto-tuned. I want to go back to the basics of music and let people fall in love with the rhythm and lyrics and not so much the show I put on. There's something about sitting on stage and performing without the loud amplifiers and flashy light shows. I want people to feel the intimacy that music can provide.

I search through my purse for my ringing phone. When I see who's calling, I know my face is beaming. "Hello," I answer with pure excitement.

Ryan laughs on the other end. "I was going to ask what you're doing, but I can hear."

"I'm fascinated, what can I say."

"Hmm, you can say you'll meet me at the stadium in an hour or so."

I look at my watch and see that it's now rush hour. The trains will be jam packed. "An hour is doable, I think. It just depends on the trains."

"It's fine, I can wait. Just get here, okay?"

"Okay, on my way. I love you." I smile brightly as the last three words roll off my tongue. Telling him that I love him has to be my most satisfying achievement each and every day.

"I love you too, Hadley," he replies before hanging up. As much as I hate leaving before their show is done, I'm more eager to see Ryan. I pull a few twenties out of my wallet and set them in their bucket. I've spoken to a few of these guys and know that they work minimum wage jobs and do this to put a little more food on the table. A couple of the guys bring their little kids down to watch so that they're working but still

with family. Seeing this makes me very thankful for what my parents did for me.

I hustle to the train, longing to see Ryan. There isn't a game tonight and it does strike me as odd that we didn't make plans. Not that we need to see each other every night, but I'm not complaining if we do. The break-up, while it hurt, did us well. We were able to grow, function normally without being dependent upon each other and fall in love all over again. I think that has been our biggest blessing, love. I now find myself craving him. The need to be near him is so great that each time I see him, I'm warm and tingly and feel like I'm falling all over again. It's a feeling I never want to lose.

By time I'm at the stop for the ballpark, I'm only ten minutes late. I rush down the hall and up the escalator to his office. I bypass his receptionist, Wendy, who I found out is Jessica's best friend. Since Ryan and I started dating, she's been cordial, but can't get over the fact that Ryan and Jessica broke up because of me. I know Jessica has told her that's not the case and if she and I can be friends, surely her best friend can get over it. No such luck.

When I get to Ryan's office, his lights are off. Reluctantly, I have to ask Wendy where he is, and this never goes well. I stop in front of her desk and paste a nice fake smile on my face. "Hi, Wendy, can you tell me where Ryan is?"

She rolls her eyes and doesn't hide her distaste for me. "Mr. Stone asked that you meet him on the field. If you follow -"

"I know the way, thank you," I cut her off before she can finish. I'm growing impatient and don't understand why he wouldn't be in his office.

As soon as I'm through the tunnel that separates the field from the club house, I spot Ryan standing on the pitcher's mound. I climb the steps slowly and step out onto the warning track.

"Hey, Hadley."

"Hey, Ryan."

"Why don't you come here for a minute?"

I nod and step onto the grass, hopping over the white chalked lines. Usually the field is covered so the rain doesn't

damage the grass, but today, it's open like a playground. I want to take off my shoes and run, but I refrain.

Reaching Ryan, he pulls me into his arms and kisses me deeply. "Turn around," he says, but doesn't release me. He faces us in the direction of the jumbotron, the same one where we're caught on the "kiss cam".

"I love you, Hadley," he whispers in my ear as music starts playing. Tears well in my eyes as a slideshow starts. There are images of us when we were babies and growing up and finally of us together, even when he was seventeen. I wrap my arms around him, leaning into his shoulder.

"I love this."

"Me too, but it's not over."

The music changes into *Canon in D* as the words "Will You Marry Me?" appear on the screen. I gasp and cover my mouth as the tears flow. I turn in his arms and nod feverishly, words escaping me in this very important moment.

Ryan sighs. "Is that a yes?"

"Yes! Yes! Yes!"

"Phew, I was getting a little worried." Only he would make light of an important moment like this. "So, I was thinking we'd get married tonight."

"What?" I deadpan.

He moves a few steps to the right to show me what's going on behind him. My parents, his mom, Alex, Cole and Hayden, Dylan and her daughter, Carrie, and a few of our friends are all standing at home plate.

"What's going on?" I ask.

Ryan shrugs. "Well, from the looks of it, we're getting married tonight."

"Right here?"

"Is there a better place?"

I shake my head. "No there isn't, but how? We don't have a marriage license."

Ryan runs his hand through his hair. "Minor technicality that Carrie was able to fix for us. I assure you, if we get married right now, it'll be legal."

"So, what are we waiting for?" As soon as I say those

words, music queues up again and Ryan takes my hand in his arm and walks us to home plate. Our friends and family move aside and a minister appears ready to make us official.

In only a few short minutes, with traditional vows exchanged, Ryan and I are husband and wife, and while this may be the most nontraditional wedding in the history of nontraditional weddings, the fact that it's mine makes it the most perfect.

chapter
fourteen

RYAN

Ask me nine years ago, when I was sitting on my bed listening to my best friend, Dylan, go on and on about the concert tickets she won, if I thought I'd meet my wife that night, the answer would be a resounding no. I owe so much to Dylan – even if she refuses to acknowledge her part in my life when it comes to Hadley – that I'll never be able to repay her. Yes, some of the best and also most troubling times in my life are because of Hadley, but I wouldn't trade them for anything. Nothing can compare to what I'm feeling now that I've heard the minister tell me that I may now kiss my bride.

The moment our lips connect, I know I made the right decision by surprising her with this wedding. Getting everyone here was a challenge, especially Dylan, who was adamant that I'm making a mistake. Thing is, it's my mistake to make. I didn't tell her that her daughter, Emma, was a mistake or that she needed to marry that sorry excuse for a father. I supported

her and expect the same in return. Cole and Alex were the easy part. Alex was beyond excited and swore she wouldn't say anything. Cole told me he was happy that everything was working out the way it should be. The fact that he thought Hadley and I belonged together makes me appreciate him even more as a friend.

Rebuilding our lives together these past months has been perfect and exciting. Hadley will be finishing out the tour she cancelled when she showed up in my office and as much as I don't want her to leave, it's better that she's doing it when I'm back to work. We're taking a month off after the season ends and going far away to some tropical island where cell phones don't work. We haven't decided yet where that is, and I've threatened that we'll end up at the airport and looking at the reader board, still trying to decide. I don't care where, as long as she's with me.

"I now pronounce you Mr. and Mrs. Ryan Stone," the minister says to the happy delights of our family. I can even hear Dylan clapping behind me. Someday, I know she'll get over her hate for Hadley.

I cup Hadley's face and watch as tears pool. "You're my wife… finally," I add the last part with jest and earn a smile from her.

"I can't believe you did all of this without me knowing."

I look around and see the many shining faces of our family. "Everyone knew, except you. I didn't want to plan anything and I wanted it to be special, something we can tell our kids when they're older. I want us to be as spontaneous as our careers allow."

"I like that a lot, Ryan. I love you so much."

I shake my head. "Not nearly as much as I love you, and speaking of spontaneity, I have another surprise for you."

Hadley's eyes light up. "What is it?"

I glower at her. "A surprise, Hadley," I say, shaking my head. I take her by the hand and lead her into the dugout. Everyone will meet us later after I do this one last thing.

As soon as we're out of the stadium, I stop and spin her around.

"What's my surprise, Ryan? I'm not seeing anything." Her voice is frantic. I know she's thinking that she missed something, but she hasn't.

I pull a blindfold out of my pocket and cover her eyes. Leaning in I whisper, "It's not here." Taking her hand in mine, I lead her to the waiting limo and help her climb in.

"You don't have to surprise me with a reception. I know those usually follow weddings," she says with a huff. I stifle a laugh, which turns into a full-blown laughing fit when she turns and tries to glare at me. Her brows are furrowed and I can only imagine what her eyes look like right now. I take this opportunity to kiss her, letting my lips linger on hers until I can melt away her anger. When I taste her, it takes every ounce of self-control to not pull her into my lap and have my way with her. It wouldn't be the first time we've had sex in a limo. We've had plenty of miles added over the years. However, our first time as husband and wife will be in our new home, which I'm about to show her now.

The limo pulls up and the driver is out his door and opening ours before I can even fathom that we're now homeowners. I found a small cape with cedar shingle siding and couldn't pass it up. The house in on Cape Cod, and while my commute to work will be the death of me, waking up and seeing the ocean every morning is a reward. I'm hoping that Hadley can find inspiration here and that maybe the pitter-patter of baby feet will make their arrival soon.

I guide her to the front of the house and hold her in my arms. The back of her head rests on my shoulder while her hands hang off my arms. I glance at her ring, a new one that I bought only a few days ago, and realize it's more perfect than the first one.

"I hear the ocean, Ry."

"I know," I say as I slip of her blindfold. She gasps and covers her mouth with her hand.

"Welcome home, Mrs. Stone."

Hadley turns in my arms, again with tears in her eyes and leaps. My arms encase her as her lips crash down on mine. I use this to my advantage and carry her up the stairs. My mom

left the door unlocked earlier so I wouldn't have to fumble with the keys. I open the door and pull her away from me, only to pick her up bridal style so I can carry her over the threshold.

Inside, the living room is empty, as well as the kitchen and two of the three bedrooms. I stand back and watch as she surveys the rooms. Her fingers leaving a trail with each part of the house that she touches.

"You didn't decorate or move your stuff in?"

I shake my head. "No, I thought we could start anew."

Her smile brightens as she turns to walk down the hall. I follow, leaving a few steps in between.

"Ryan, there's a bed in here."

I take the last few steps and pause, leaning up against the doorjamb. "I may have ordered us a bed."

"And why would you do something like that?"

"Oh, I don't know, Hadley," I say, stepping into the room. "The thought of making love to my wife, on our wedding day, in our new house, on a nice firm bed really appeals to me."

I shut the door behind me and get lost in the beauty that is before me. When I met Hadley Carter, she changed my world. At the time, I didn't know if it would be for better or for worse, but from here on out, I know that nothing can be better than sharing my life with my soul mate. Hadley may write songs about falling in love and even breaking up, but standing here with her in front of me as she slowly strips out of her clothes, brings me to a place I never thought I'd be. She's undressing for the first time as my wife in our new home. Each step I take toward her is calculated with no risk involved. She's not going to deny me, and it's not because I'm her husband. It's because she loves me with her whole being.

My fingers reach out to caress her skin and I chuckle, watching her flesh pebble. Hadley quickly works the buttons of my dress shirt, eager for me to be in the same undressed state that she's in. A few months ago, I would've appeased her and shed all my clothes, but not now. This is the moment that she and I will be lost in us, forever.

ABOUT THE AUTHOR

Her grandma once told her that she can do anything she wants, so she is. Originally from the Pacific Northwest, she now lives in picturesque Vermont, with her husbnad and two daughters. Also renting space in their home is an overhyper Beagle/Jack Russell and two parakeets.

During the day you'll find her behind a desk talking about Land Use. At night, she's writing one of the many stories she plans to release or sitting courtside during either daughter's basketball games.

Shes's also an active book reviewer on The Readiacs.

Find Heidi on:

Twitter: twitter.com/HeidiJoVT
Facebook: www.facebook.com/HeidiMcLaughlinAuthor
or her Blog: heidimclaughlinauthor.blogspot.com/

This paperback interior was designed and formatted by

E.M. TIPPETTS

BOOK DESIGNS

www.emtippettsbookdesigns.com

Artisan interiors for discerning authors and publishers.

Other Books by Heidi McLaughlin

Lost in You

The Beaumont Series:

Forever My Girl - #1
My Everything - #1.5
My Unexpected Forever - #2
Finding My Forever - #3
Finding My Way - #4

LOST

IN

US

HEIDI MCLAUGHLIN

LOST

IN

US